GRACIE La Roo
ON THE BIG SCREEN

written by **MARSHA QUALEY**
illustrated by **KRISTYNA LITTEN**

PICTURE WINDOW BOOKS
a capstone imprint

Gracie LaRoo on the Big Screen is published by
Picture Window Books, a Capstone imprint
1710 Roe Crest Drive
North Mankato, MN 56003
www.mycapstone.com

Library of Congress Cataloging-in-Publication data is
available on the Library of Congress website.

Summary: Gracie finds her voice and makes her debut
as a spinning, dazzling, mertail-wearing actress.

ISBN 978-1-5158-1441-2 (library binding)
ISBN 978-1-5158-1445-0 (ebook pdf)

Designer: Aruna Rangarajan

Editor: Megan Atwood

Production Specialist: Steve Walker

Printed and bound in the USA
010401F17

TABLE OF CONTENTS

GRACIE and The

NAME: Gracie LaRoo

TEAM: Water Sprites

CLAIM TO FAME:
Being the youngest pig to join a world-renowned synchronized swimming team!

SIGNATURE MOVE:
"When Pigs Fly" Spin

LIKES: Purple, clip-on tail bows, mud baths, newly mown hay smell

DISLIKES: Too much attention, doing laundry, scary movies

QUOTE

"I just hope I can be the kind of synchronized swimmer my team needs!"

WATER SPRITES

JINI

BARB

JIA

SU

MARTHA

BRADY

SILVIA

HOG HEAVEN

Gracie LaRoo stared at the big red building.

Hog Heaven Studios.

She shivered with excitement and nerves. She was going to be in a movie with Tilda Swinetune, the champion swim racer and movie star!

"I wish the other Water Sprites were here with me," she whispered to herself. "Then I wouldn't be nervous at all."

A very tall sow burst through a door.

Gracie recognized Mira Patel, the most famous movie director in Piggywood.

The director reached Gracie and bowed. She said, "At last you are here! I am humbled to meet the water ballet champion, Gracie LaRoo!"

Gracie couldn't speak. No one had ever bowed to her before. Especially someone famous.

Mira said, "I have watched the wonderful PigTube videos of your team. The Wiggly Piggly Pyramid! The Train of Trotters! But your spins are what dazzle me. I knew I must have you in the movie. Did you receive the movie script?"

Gracie nodded. "I read it on the plane," she said. "Which part is for me? I know Tilda is the Queen, but — "

Mira cut her off. "Come inside and see your stage!"

THE SUIT

It was the biggest swimming pool Gracie had ever seen.

Mira said, "Go peek. There is just a rehearsal going on."

Gracie climbed a ladder to see it all.

Eight pigs in bright colored suits were in the water. Someone shouted, "One . . .two . . . three!"

One by one the swimmers dove, flipping up fishtails as their heads disappeared underwater.

Those are the merpigs! Gracie thought. Since reading the script, Gracie had hoped she would be a merpig in the movie.

She also hoped her

costume would be purple.

"Mira Patel, we have

to talk!" A voice called out.

It was Tilda Swinetune!

Gracie climbed down the ladder.

Tilda strode forward. She did

not look happy.

Mira trotted toward Tilda, "Gracie La Roo has arrived. Now the movie will be dazzling!"

Tilda looked at Gracie. "Her? I know she's a water ballet star, but she's hardly more than a piglet!"

"But have you seen her spin?" Mira asked. "We can film her and make it look like you!"

No one will even know I'm in the movie? Gracie thought unhappily. Her shoulders slumped.

Mira moved closer to Tilda.

"Just picture it: the merpig queen
is captured by pirates. But she
escapes! She celebrates by leaping
off the rocks into a circle of her
cheering merpigs. Dazzling!"

Tilda put her hooves on her hips. "I am the fastest swimmer in the world. Why isn't speed part of the story? That's dazzling!"

Mira said, "Just wait until you see her fly. Then you'll understand!"

She shouted to the movie crew, "Put Gracie in the suit!"

GRACIE'S VISION

Gracie wanted to cry. "I have to wear this?" she said and snuffled a little.

"When you wear that suit," Mira said, "our special camera films your movement. Then we add Tilda's face and costume when we edit the movie."

She smiled. "When the audience sees the spin, they'll think she's the one doing your trick. Movie magic!"

Gracie thought, *I really wanted to be a merpig.*

The director pointed to the big pile of rocks and said, "Up you go."

Gracie looked at the very highest rock. She said, "You want me to leap from there?"

"Leap and spin," Mira said. "The flat rock on top is fake. Inside are two springs. The top of that rock will pop up and push you high into the air."

Tilda grumble-oinked. Then she sat in a chair and groinked once more.

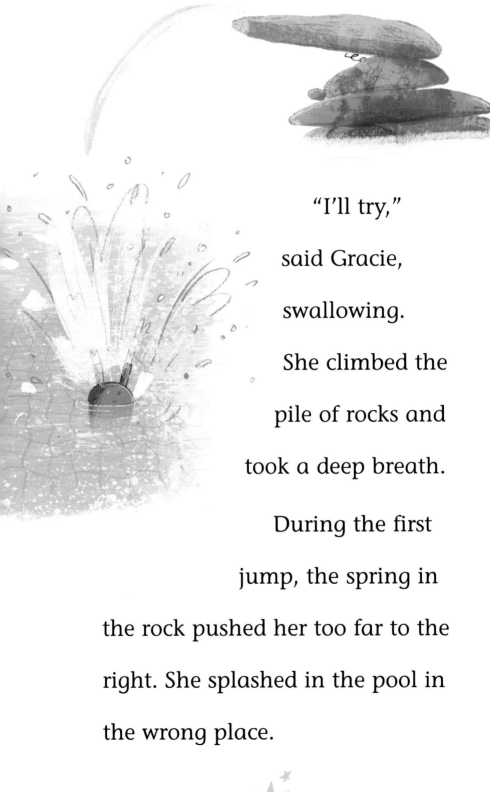

"I'll try," said Gracie, swallowing. She climbed the pile of rocks and took a deep breath. During the first jump, the spring in the rock pushed her too far to the right. She splashed in the pool in the wrong place.

The second time, the spring in the rock pushed her too far to the left. She splashed in the wrong place again.

Gracie climbed out of the pool and wiped water from her eyes. "Maybe if we — "

Tilda interrupted. "This will never work," she said to Mira.

"It must work!" Mira said. "Her spins will make my movie sensational!"

As they argued, Gracie climbed up the ladder and stared at the beautiful pool with the big pirate ship.

What if the pirates captured a merpig instead of the queen? she thought. *Then the queen could lead the pirates on a chase. That way, everyone could see how fast Tilda is!*

The angry voices below her
grew even louder.

Gracie climbed down the
rocks. "Please stop arguing!" she
said. No one paid attention.

"I have an idea," she said a
little louder.

But the argument between Mira and Tilda got louder too.

Gracie took a big breath and shouted, "LISTEN TO ME!"

Everyone turned in surprise.

Gracie smiled and said to the whole crew, "I know what to do."

CHAPTER 4

DAZZLING!

The theater was full. The lights dimmed. The screen grew bright.

Gracie wiggled with excitement. She smiled to herself in the dark theater. She couldn't wait for her part: the smallest merpig, captured by the pirates! She concentrated on the movie.

The merpigs swam around the queen, who was Tilda Swinetune. She wore a necklace with a huge pearl in it.

The pirate ship came into the picture. Gracie couldn't stop herself from gasping. The ship looked so much bigger on the screen.

"They want the pearl! Dive deep and swim to the caves!" yelled the queen to the merpigs.

On the screen, the camera showed a little pig in a purple mertail, flopping in a net. A pirate called out, "Too late! Give us the pearl or we'll sell your friend to a circus!"

Gracie wanted to explode with excitement. SHE was the little merpig captured. She even got to wear the purple mertail!

The queen gasped. "We must summon help from our sea friends."

An octopus appeared on the screen and threw the queen high in the air. The queen did one, two, three spins and landed on the deck of the ship.

Tilda turned in her seat and winked at Gracie. That had really been Gracie in the green suit rolling through the air. Movie magic!

After the queen freed Gracie

the merpig from the ship, she

slipped into the water to escape.

The pirates caught sight of

her. She yelled, "If you want the

pearl, try to catch me!"

The pirates tried to catch the queen, but she swam in circles—and led the ship right into a rock!

Crash!

The queen joined her merpigs in the moonlit water, Gracie the merpig right by her side.

THE END scrawled across the screen.

The lights went up. The audience cheered and clapped.

Gracie rose with the other
actors and took a big bow. She had
become a movie star!

Tilda leaned over and whispered in Gracie's ear, "Thank you, my little flying pig."

Gracie kissed the famous actress on her cheek and then spun around three times in her purple gown.

GLOSSARY

concentrate — to focus on something

dazzling — exciting!

gasping — to breathe in a quick breath

grumble — to complain in a low voice

humbled — to feel grateful

merpig — part mermaid, part pig

nerves — being worried or anxious

scrawled — to write

sensational — amazing!

snuffled — to sniff sadly

trotted — to jog lightly

TALK ABOUT IT!

1. Can you think of a movie that had special effects or had "movie magic?"

2. Why did Tilda and Mira argue?

3. What would you have done if you were in Gracie's place?

WRITE ABOUT IT!

1. Write a movie starring Gracie. What would her story be?

2. Write a letter from Tilda to Mira, explaining why she wanted the movie to show her speed.

3. Write an email from Gracie to the Water Sprites. What would she tell them about her experience making the movie?

About the Author

Marsha Qualey is the author of many books for readers young and old. Though she learned to swim when she was very young, she says she has never tried any of the moves and spins Gracie does so well.

Marsha has four grown-up children and two grandchildren. She lives in Wisconsin with her husband and their two non-swimming cats.

Kristyna Litten is an award winning children's book illustrator and author. After studying illustration at Edinburgh College of Art, she now lives and works from Yorkshire in the UK, with her pet rabbit Herschel.

Kristyna would not consider herself a very good swimmer as she can only do the breaststroke, but when she was younger, she would do a tumble roll and a handstand in the shallow end of the pool.

THE WONDERFUL, THE AMAZING, THE PIG-TASTIC GRACIE LAROO!

Discover more at
www.capstonekids.com

- Find out more about Gracie and her adventures.

- Follow the Water Sprites as they craft their routines.

- Figure out what you would do . . . if you were the awesome Gracie LaRoo!